M000221319

Praise

"The stories in *Automatically Hip*, John McCaffrey's latest collection, are funny, irreverent and imbued with creative soul."
SCOTT HAMILTON-KENNEDY, ACADEMY AWARD® NOMINEE

"*Automatically Hip* begins with a story of Thelonious Monk and then applies the jazz legend's improvisational technique to prose. McCaffrey's vignettes are jazzy riffs on the quieter moments of human connection. They are musical, surprising, and a pleasure."
IRIS SMYLES, AUTHOR OF *DATING TIPS FOR THE UNEMPLOYED*

"If you haven't read one of John McCaffrey's stories, you're in for a treat. John consistently looks at things carefully and originally. He describes them thoughtfully, and never ceases to surprise his reader with unexpected, yet earned outcomes. His attention to language, fine dialogue, and high-level character development is dependably excellent and simply a pleasure. Take a look at the first story, and title of the book, *Automatically Hip*. I'm sure you'll eagerly want to read all of John's refreshing, always enjoyable work."
BURT WEISSBOURD, AUTHOR OF *DANGER IN PLAIN SIGHT*

"John McCaffrey's *Automatically Hip* is an amazing, compact, powerful and insightful plunge into the collective loneliness, and the disjointed togetherness, of our tattered country. His fourteen brief but breathtaking stories reassure us that there are people still out there searching for something—and in today's chaotic, fractured world, the search is all that matters. McCaffrey is truly an old-school storyteller in a post-modern world, who captures the unsteadiness of our age with great humor and compassion. Pick up this book, dear reader, and brace yourself—these stories come fast, and each one packs a sweet little punch."

FRANK HABERLE, AUTHOR OF *SHUFFLERS*

"McCaffrey has deviated from the idiosyncratic to gift us with vignettes of brief, human warmness. The multitude of voices in *Automatically Hip* speak to us in one magnificent language; empathy and compassion."

ERIK RASCHKE, AUTHOR OF *THE BOOK OF SAMUEL*

About the Author

Originally from Rochester, New York, John McCaffrey attended Villanova University and received his M.A. in Creative Writing from the City College of New York. He is the author of *TheBook of Ash*, a science fiction novel, and the short story collections *Two Syllable Men* and *What's Wrong With This Picture?*. Nominated multiple times for a PushcartPrize, he teaches creative writing in New York City, and is a columnist for The Good Men Project.

www.jamccaffrey.com

JOHN MCCAFFREY

Automatically Hip

Automatically Hip
Copyright © 2022 John McCaffrey
All rights reserved.

Print Edition
ISBN: 978-1-925965-94-0
Published by Vine Leaves Press 2022

No parts of this publication may be reproduced, stored in a retrieval system, or transmitted in any form or by any means, electronic, mechanical, photocopying, recording, or otherwise, without the prior written permission of the copyright owner.

This book is sold subject to the condition that it shall not, by way of trade or otherwise, be lent, resold, hired out, or otherwise circulated without the publisher's prior consent in any form of binding or cover other than that in which it is published and without a similar condition including this condition being imposed on the subsequent purchaser. Under no circumstances may any part of this book be photocopied for resale.

This is a work of fiction. Any similarity between the characters and situations within its pages and places or persons, living or dead, is unintentional and coincidental.

Cover design by Jessica Bell
Interior design by Amie McCracken

NATIONAL
LIBRARY
OF AUSTRALIA

A catalogue record for this book is available from the National Library of Australia

For Grace

Automatically Hip

AUTHOR'S NOTE: In August 1951, police arrested jazz pianist Thelonious Monk for possession of heroin that wasn't his. He spent sixty days in prison and lost his New York cabaret card, forcing him to play in obscurity for the next several years.

IF YOU PLAY jazz with cats, whether they're finger zingers or rusty gates, no matter if they have balloon lungs or freak lips, if the rhythm is gut bucket or smoking, you're bound to throw out a clunker or have one passed your way now and again. It's a lot like life: everyone hits or gets a bad note from time-to-time, a moment when you put something negative onto someone else or they, as the Bible says, do the same onto you. Well, maybe that's not how it exactly goes in the Good Book. But when you're on a stage in front of folks who dropped more than a few hard-earned dimes to hear a sugar band, and you're the lead, the star, the one they all came to see, and you get blown a change from a licorice stick or a rat-a-tat from a tub that makes you wish you hadn't turned down before that puff of muggle, that cool shot of M., when all of a sudden the air leaves the room and there is no conceivable way to make sense, much less music, from the hand you've been dealt ... that, I tell you, is the moment when genius is not forged, but revealed; when you can turn death into breath, restart the heart and reorder the world, so that everything sounds just like it should, a balance of smooth and static, up and down, back and forth, mute to murmur, a pleasing-to-the-ear disconnect that bothers your nerves and makes you wonder why you're so plain and wooden in the presence of such greatness. And none of it would be possible, this creation of pristine artistry, this prurient display of unfettered brilliance, this "thank the dear Lord I decided to come tonight" moment, without that bad note, that clunker.

If you think by my language I'm a Jazz fan, you're right. But if you think I'm part of that world, part of the swarm, part of a humming hive of men and women who move to a beat that doesn't always follow a beat, then you're wrong. I'm just not welcome inside the circle, and not because of race (I'm white Irish) or anything cliché like that, and not because I can't play a lick on any instrument made by man or forged through God's good graces, and not because I don't understand what Jazz truly is, the essence of it, the soul of it, because I think I do. I don't even think it's because I'm a cop, or a retired cop, which is what I am now. But because I was a cop, back in 1951, working for the narcotics division, creeping around in a cruiser one night, in a Harlem neighborhood where we were told to creep around, and we saw two guys sitting in a parked car, minding their own business, and we decided to make it our business. I wish now I had recognized the man at the wheel; I should have. I'd seen him play a few times, or should I say I'd heard him play a few times because that was what hit you first and hardest, the sound of his piano; you never heard anyone play like that, I assure you. He did something to your ears, made them happy and sad and wishing they were bigger the moment he put his fingers to the keys. But I didn't recognize him, and when we spotted the heroin it was all too late; soon the two men were at Rikers, and I sealed my place in history: I had arrested Thelonious Monk.

You might think me a coward for not telling the cops it was my heroin, for letting my best friend take the fall, the long-term pinch. But you have to know Monk wouldn't let me admit that it was my bag, wouldn't let me take responsibility for the junk. He actually forbade me to speak up, something made clear to me that night in the car, and every day for the next seven years he was exiled from the stage. Even when I begged him to let me come clean, he'd say, in that warm and weary voice, "No, Buddy, the beat stops with me."

It's quite a thing to feel guilty about for such a long time. It's like having a low-grade fever; not bad enough to stay in bed all day, but you wish you could. You just never feel good, even when you think you've forgotten what troubles you, when the moment you're in is sweet and fine and you think you have found heaven here on earth. That's when it jumps up and lets you know you're not free to have such pleasure, the thought pulling you down so fast from the perch you were on it's like you have vertigo, like you jumped out of a window on the way to meet your maker. But you never land, you never die, and you never get over the bad feeling. Like a low-grade fever, I tell you. Just like it.

Maybe the first year was the best, only because I was around Monk a lot and riding the injustice of the whole thing. I felt like we were still in it together, that the cops were the enemies, and that I wasn't a snitch. Monk was in my corner, assuring me I had not done wrong by keeping my mouth shut. He wouldn't let anyone talk dirty about me either, at least not around his sharp ears. But they did, friends and foes alike put me down as yellow and spineless, a weak person, a bad seed. It started to get to me, and when it did, the itch for drugs was strong. I was done though, with heroin. I couldn't even say the word without feeling repulsed after what it had done to me and to Monk. So I did other things, and there were always other things to do.

But nothing gave me that same glaze, that feeling of being dead to the world. Heroin made my mind drift like a balloon tied to a body stuck in cement. The funny thing was that even smoked to the gills, I could make my fingers dance. Maybe my feet felt like lead, but my hands never had trouble until that night I tried to toss the baggie out the window and missed, dropping the damn thing right at Monk's feet for the cops to find. Some people said that if I only had been straight I would have tossed the thing right and we'd be cleared, but I never had problems with my hands before, gassed or not. This, you see, was really about aim.

Once the fire burned down, once people got used to the idea that I was no good, that I was scared to take what was owed to me, that I gave the time I couldn't do to my friend to do, then I burned down too. I lost my spark. I simmered in my own juices. I shuffled around with head down, like a beaten man not allowed to admit he's beaten. I blame Monk for that. Yes, I do. I got him into a jam and he wouldn't let me get him out of it, which kept me in it. The way I see it, Monk took a bullet for me, and after that I took a bomb for him. I let him take and hold the high ground while I rolled downhill those seven years they forcibly exiled him from the stage.

Now, those that know about Monk, fans who have followed his history, will shout out that either they saw him play when he was banned from doing such,

at least in New York, or heard that he had taken
some stage in disguise, under an alias, with his fellow musicians sworn to secrecy. The word was he
did this to keep his jazz muscle honed, to get a few
dollars, even to lift his spirits. Well, it's true. Monk
did play to audiences those years, but not for the
reasons most felt. He did it because it was the right
note to play next, the right way to take the clunker
he got from me and extend it so it would become,
one day, part of a perfect, pristine, gorgeous set. You
see, most people don't realize that Monk saw everything in life as a piece of music; everything to him
was jazz. That was his true genius. There was no
separation to his art: he was jazz, jazz was him. So
when that bag of H landed at his feet, he reacted the
same way as when sitting at the piano and the skins
missed a beat: he took in the information, made a
decision on how to get the joint jumping again, and
then did it. In this case it meant taking responsibility for the junk, sending me into a guilty spiral, and
waiting out seven years until it cleared. Ah, you say,
but he played for the public during that time. Yes,
and no. He played, but not as Monk; what I'm saying is he held back his talent, suppressing all the
magic that made his sound so unique, so impactful.
This was part of the set, keeping a blanket on the
beauty, manifesting, if you will, a seven-year flu.
When I would listen to a set he played during that
time, and I was always there when he slipped on a

stage, it reminded me of a basketball player I knew, a cat named Jack Molinas who lit it up at Columbia right around the time Monk and I got busted. Jack was a Jewish kid with a handsome face and a jones for gambling. He threw games, dumped them, shaved points, and made a bundle from bookies. If you watched Jack play straight up, he would dismantle all and everyone, pros and asphalt legends. But when you watched him when he "worked," when he played for the illegal buck, you winced in pain, your soul longing to see that athletic machine performing at one hundred percent. That's how it was when I watched Monk play during that time. I could not help but wince as well, to run out of the place screaming and howling, for I knew I was the reason this was going on, and I knew he wanted it to go on.

Finally, my anguish stopped. New York State, one day, cleared him. Gave him back his name, and his game. And like a crocus that rises overnight from a thawing soil, Monk appeared on stage: walked right out, sat at the piano, and without introduction, without looking at the audience, without even a nod of the head, began to play all the way.

My father was a man who spoke just loud enough to make you lean forward to hear what he said. It wasn't as if he was holding back volume intentionally, for impact or effect, and I wouldn't call him soft-spoken, because his words, whatever the decibel level, had a unique bite to them, a sting even, like getting a shot from the doctor, a fast prick letting you know you've been connected with the medicine, and then the pain is gone—just like that—and it's in your veins doing the work. I was young when it happened: when he got in trouble with my Uncle Buddy and couldn't play. You have to know I didn't really understand much of what happened, and I didn't really care as long as he wasn't in jail and taken away from me. On that end, those seven years he was silent, as I like to call it now, were probably the best seven years of my life, only because he was home an awful lot, and being at home he was with me an awful lot, which was not awful at all.

What I liked about my father was his inability to treat me as anything but a level-headed person. No matter the inane things that came from my child's mouth, the petty rages that befall all boys when they try to flex intellectual and emotional muscles not yet developed, the constant tug at his sleeve to include me in all and everything in his life, no matter what I did or didn't do, when he talked to me, when he leveled that amazing gaze and took me in, I believe he saw me as an equal, and as an equal, he would not suffer me as a fool.

I know he didn't like being around the house sometimes; my mother and he would fight. Not terrible arguments, no screaming and throwing of items in grasping distance, which is something I heard in other apartments in our building, but little scraps, which is the best way I could describe, quick-hitting barbs toward each other and an occasional shaken fist or pantomimed slap to the face. Money was an issue: my mom was always worried about meeting household expenses, and my father was always indifferent to her worry, which made her even madder. But I don't remember ever missing a meal those seven years, or the lights going off, or not getting a coat when I needed one, or some change to run out and buy ice cream. I'd like to think my father was a hustler—would figure out ways to make bread when he couldn't really do what he was put on Earth to do, what, I believe, God wanted him to do, to play music that no one played before. I knew he hauled furniture now and again, helped people move, cleaned out homes and basements, even drove trucks. I also know he played a few gigs: I'd see him leave home and know right away; not his clothes, but his gait, the carry of his head, the bounce, told me at least he was heading toward the music. One time I followed him, snuck out and trailed him all the way to Harlem, to a little place he ducked in. I remember seeing Uncle Buddy outside, and another guy, a white man with a big, red, sad face. He struck me because I'd seen him hanging around outside our apartment a few times over the years, with the same hangdog expression. I overheard my mother once say he was a cop.

When I started to get older and began to realize what had happened, and with my growing sense of self, I became more concerned about myself. Basically, I worried that whatever happened to my father would pass on to me; that no one would take me seriously as a musician, which is what I had decided to become. I remember when I leveled that at my father, he smiled, and then, with a flutter of fingers in the air, as if he was about to lay them on the keys, said, "Don't worry, you're my son. You're automatically hip." It made me feel better, and then it made me feel nervous because I didn't know what hip really was, didn't know what it really felt like. But he did, and he knew it could carry through to another generation; just to be sure, when those seven years were up, when they welcomed him back, he made sure to transform into the real Thelonious Monk the hippest way possible: quietly.

If you really want to know the real story, what I felt, why I did what I did, why I didn't do what I could, listen. Listen close. It's the only way.

Building A

IT WAS LATE morning when Bill, the crew's foreman, collapsed. He was a heavy man with a ruddy face and fingers as thick as blood sausages. He fell headfirst into a stack of metal piping. Blood trickled from his forehead.

Henry, hauling cement for the foundation that would become Building A, dropped his wheelbarrow and sped over with several others to check on Bill.

"Is he okay?" he asked.

Chuck, who ran the mixer, was kneeling over the stricken man.

"He's breathing. Call 911."

Willie, the union guy, who earlier had told the men about a new dental plan, eased a cell phone from his belt. He dialed and ordered the ambulance.

"It's coming," he said in a cigarette-scarred voice. "Don't move him."

"I know not to move him," Chuck snapped back.

"It looks like you wanted to."

"You're wrong."

They waited in silence until the ambulance came.

Two paramedics spilled out with a stretcher on wheels.

"How long has he been unconscious?" the taller of the two inquired.

Willie checked his wristwatch.

"I'd say five minutes."

"More like ten," Chuck corrected him.

The paramedics examined Bill. After, they placed him on the stretcher, brought him back to the ambulance, and drove away. Never once did they turn on the siren.

"Those boys know what they're doing," Willie wheezed, fingering a cigarette from a pack in his shirt breast pocket and placing it between his lips.

"I'm sure they get a lot of practice," Chuck added.

Willie lit the cigarette, took a long drag, and then blew smoke out his nose.

"Anyone know if Bill had a bad heart?" he asked.

Chuck kicked at a rock the size of a baseball.

"He told me once he had gout."

"That wouldn't kill him."

"It hurts just the same."

Willie nodded. He took another long drag, exhaled, and spoke through the smoke cloud covering his mouth.

"I guess I'll go check on him and see about his family getting called."

One by one the men returned to their work, finishing up Building A's footprint. Henry was exhausted by the end of the day, but he felt good about his con-tribution. The cement he had hauled had been spread out in a neat, even gray, covering any imperfection in the dusty ground. Even the indent made by Bill's fall.

Gravity

THE METALLIC-SOUNDING crash startled Virginia. She stood near a squat, muscled man. He was doing bicep curls and had let the weights fall to the floor when finished.

"Sorry. I didn't see you there," he said, training an interested stare at Virginia.

Virginia blushed. She pulled back her bangs and looked away, refocusing on the chin-up machine she had been debating whether to try.

"You want help with that?"

Virginia blushed deeper.

"I don't know. I've never done it before."

"No worry. It's easy. Watch me."

The man moved past her and climbed onto the machine. In quick motion he hoisted himself up and down like a piston.

"Your turn," he said, stepping off.

Virginia realized in a panic that once on the machine he would have full view of her backside, a part of her body she felt very insecure about. It was the major reason she had joined the gym: to lose the extra weight she had gained after her divorce.

"Maybe another time."

"C'mon. I'll help you."

"I'm not sure I can do it."

"You won't know if you don't try."

"Okay."

Virginia set her jaw and stepped forward. She grabbed the machine's handles and inhaled deeply. She felt the man's hand press into the small of her back. The unexpectedness of his touch caused her to gasp.

"Now what?" she managed to get out.

"Just press up against the resistance."

Virginia did as he said, pushing with all her strength.

"That's it," he encouraged. "You're almost there."

With elbow joints buckling, Virginia made one last effort to get to the top.

"See. You made it."

Virginia felt exhilarated. She glanced over her shoulder and saw that the man stood on tiptoes, his hand still against her back.

"Now release," he said.

But Virginia held firm, basking in her triumph, the man's touch, the sudden connection. She savored this mix of feelings, wanting to remember them when later, no matter her desire, gravity would bring her back down.

Grooved Pavement

MY FATHER got me the job for the summer. I was home after graduating from college, had no money, and had yet to decide what I wanted to do with a finance degree. A family friend owned a paving company and needed extra help after winning a contract to repair a stretch of battered highway in the Finger Lakes region of Upstate New York. The company was located about fifty miles from my parent's home. My father lent me money against my first paycheck for a cheap, clean room in a local boarding house. I moved in on a Sunday night and went to work the next morning.

My job was to drive a truck. Actually, to inch it along, keeping a straight and steady line so that the man hanging in a harness to the right of the passenger side door, wielding a lathe-like machine, could cut precise grooves in the pavement. It was tedious work, and the hours passed about as fast as the truck. It made the long evenings alone in my room even harder to take. After the first week I thought about quitting. And I might have, except that Miller, the man in the harness, invited me to dinner.

It was after work, Friday, as the crew waited for paychecks. Once they got them they left fast, except Miller, who took a long time studying the check before folding it neatly into his pocket. He came over and said: "You're welcome to eat dinner with my wife and I if you have nothing else planned."

I didn't and accepted.

To my surprise, Miller, unlike his stoic work persona, was animated and humorous at home. He was also gentle and kind to his wife, but also quick to tease her in a manner that clearly pleased her. I was surprised how easy it was to talk with him that evening, our conversation uninhibited and interesting. It set me in a better mood and I resolved to hang on to the job.

The rest of the summer, I ate at Miller's every Friday night. Perhaps the best part of the meal was our walks afterward. Once we helped clear the dishes, Miller and I would hike around his property. He had a few acres of woodland that bordered a private golf course. Sometimes we brought fishing rods with us, as a good-sized pond enveloped one of the greens. The pond held perch, blue-gill, and largemouth bass. Miller had a deal with the head groundskeeper: as long as golfers didn't complain about him fishing, he could do so. Miller also made sure to reward the groundskeeper with fresh fish. He'd keep a few every so often, clean them (Miller was an artist with a filet knife), and then gift them in plastic baggies filled with sage, thyme, and mint from his herb garden.

It was the kind of thing I would tell people about after I moved to New York City and took a job on Wall Street. "Miller time," my friends named these stories, when I would trot out my experiences that summer. Fishing on the golf course was one I told quite a bit. The "races" he'd stage at a local running track was another. Miller, although tall and lanky, had a peculiar fear he was overweight, and on Saturday mornings would get up early and head to the local high school track to do laps. I ran with him a few times but could never keep pace. I also was sometimes embarrassed to be with him. You see, if there was anyone else running the track, Miller would make it a point to draft behind them, no matter their speed, following them around until some silent bell would ring in his head and he would sprint past, arms skyward, as if crossing an imaginary finish line.

Even more peculiar were Miller's paintings. Nearly every bar or deli or store in that town had the same painting hanging prominently on a wall: a red elephant staring straight ahead, with a black bowler perched atop his head. When I questioned Miller about this he told me "he was the artist." He explained that several years earlier when work had dried up and left the crew on an extended break, he decided to take up painting to keep occupied. But for several days he could not come up with one idea that interested him. Finally, he had a dream about an elephant wearing a black hat and figured that was as good a subject as any to undertake. He painted about twenty of them, framed each, and gave them out as presents.

But for all Miller's oddities, it was the work he did, the grooving of pavement, that most interested my friends. I think the fascination was that it was tangible. When I first moved to the City, all of us were just starting out as stockbrokers, real estate agents, and lawyers, juvenile white-collar professionals toiling in an ethereal confusion devoid of non-money-related outcomes. Grooving pavement had purpose outside of a dollar: slots gouged on the side of the road stopped cars from sliding into ditches when it rained, and slots gouged on the side of a road warned drivers not to slide into ditches when it didn't. I spoke as if I was a vital part of the work, not letting on that my only role was to drive the truck like a lethargic automaton. It was Miller who needed to think, to keep a sharp eye on the diamond-tipped blades, making adjustments in positioning to ensure the cut was clean and consistent. I would have thought the job draining, but Miller found it relaxing, staring down at the cutting blades, the pavement.

It was Miller's wife who phoned me, many years later, to say he had died of a brain aneurism. She told me when and where the funeral would be held. She hoped I would come. She said he often spoke fondly of me. She intimated that he was sad we hadn't stayed in touch.

It was true. I only spoke to Miller a few times after that summer ended, and never did I go back to visit. Perhaps it was less about being busy than not wanting to look back. I certainly was driven to excel at my job. Plus I met a woman, got married, and had a daughter. My life was moving in an upward arc. I had money, security, and a loving family, everything I needed to be happy. The only problem was that I wasn't—at least not in a way that was lasting and satisfying. Happiness came only in short, fleeting bursts, usually following some sort of work success. My solution to the problem was to try and generate more and bigger successes, which required me to work harder, push harder, to focus on the end result, the future payoff. By the time I got the call from Miller's wife I was near a breaking point. My energy was depleted. I felt anxious, distracted, and had difficulty sleeping. Worse, I felt disconnected from family, from friends, from the happiness I craved.

The funeral was crowded. It was not sad. The priest, a fat old man with a face as red and fleshy as rare roast beef, gave a short Mass and then told funny stories about Miller. Afterwards, we all went to a nice restaurant in town and ate a buffet lunch. On the wall, of course, hung a painting of a red elephant wearing a black bowler.

I started on my way home right before sunset. Working my way through town toward the highway, I passed by the track where Miller used to run. I doubled back, parked, and headed to the oval. There was a young man circling all alone. He was tall and thin and ran with an easy grace. I envied his youth, his freedom of motion, the look of serenity on his face as he passed. He did another lap, and I slipped off my shoes and fell in behind him, my tie flapping in the wind as I ran, enjoying, at least for the moment, the steps I took, waiting for that silent bell to let me know it was time for a final push and victory.

Good Morning

"YOU REALLY should consider ..."

"What?"

But he already knew his wife's next word.

"Therapy."

"I was afraid you were going to say that."

He watched her lips spread out into a strong smile. Her high cheekbones pushed back against the morning light from the bedroom's lone window. She looked beautiful and decisive, and it scared him to the core.

"That's why you need therapy. To face your fears."

"That's the last thing I want to do."

"Who does? But it's the only way to get better."

"I'm not that bad, am I?"

She closed her eyes. Her breathing was deep and slow. He knew from the years they had been together that she was not just gathering her thoughts, but also reaffirming her resolve. When she looked back at him, he knew there was no turning back.

"We can go together, if you like. But only to start. This is a journey for you."

"And if I don't take this trip?"

"What do you think?"

He was always wary when she asked him a question in answer to his. It meant she was losing patience and getting angry.

"I think you will be disappointed."

"It's not about me."

"It feels that way."

She repeated her eyes closed and breathing routine.

"Okay," she said finally, blinking hard at him. "I don't want you to go to therapy."

He bit at his lower lip before answering, "I'm too old to be baited by reverse psychology."

"I mean it. I don't want you to go to therapy."

"You're lying."

"I'm not. I changed my mind. I'm allowed to do that, you know."

"I don't believe you."

"I don't care. That's my decision. And I don't want to talk about it anymore."

She left the bed, put on a housecoat, and walked out of the room and down the stairs. He heard her movements below: making coffee, opening blinds, turning on the television.

He sat up after a few moments, listening and thinking. Finally, he found his phone on the end table and did a quick search. He dialed a number and waited.

"Good morning, how can we help you today?" a friendly voice answered.

He closed his eyes, took in some deep breaths.

"Yes, hello," the voice continued.

"Hi, sorry," he said, opening his eyes. "I wanted to inquire about therapy."

Frost Fish

FROST FISH, herring as long as a tall man's hand, once littered this beach in winter. On freezing nights. Full moons. High tides. Still and stiff atop the cold sand. Their silver bodies shining like fallen stars.

"They school offshore in the warmer water," I tell Anne. "But striped bass and other predator fish herd them toward the beach where it's colder. Once they hit this current they go numb. It knocks them out. Then the waves wash them in. All we have to do is scoop them up."

Anne is short and thin with skin paler than the snow-dusted sand crunching under our boots. She's nearly opaque, her veins a faint green beneath the skin.

"I'm scared," she says, her voice childlike, pleading. "The water's too close."

The ocean crowds us, the waves crashing hard under pressure from the full moon and high tide. We approach a man-made jetty, its boulder-size black rocks scarred by the dynamite that set them in place. It starts half-buried in beach sand and vanishes fifty yards out into the churning Atlantic.

"Don't be a baby," I say. "Just look at the moon-light on the water. It's worth the cold to see this. It's beautiful ... right?"

Anne doesn't answer. She hunches under her hood and hugs her shoulders. I walk fast and motion for her to keep pace. My breath spills from my mouth in patches of mist. Fog rises from the roiling surf.

"Why?" Anne inquires about the fog.

"Because the water is warmer than the air," I explain.

"Oh," she says. Then, "How much further?"

"Not much. C'mon. You'll appreciate it later. When we get back home. The warm house will feel great. Some hot tea. Trust me."

"I don't see any fish," Anne says. She's holding a plastic grocery bag to put the herring in. "Let's go. My face is freezing."

"Hand me the light."

Anne reaches into her parka, pulls out a flashlight, and hands it over.

I switch it on and scan the beach. The light shines a sickly yellow against the clear sand. I run the beam to the surf and back, checking between the jetty rocks. No frostfish. I point the light at Anne. She's shivering and bouncing in place.

"Can we go now?"

The ocean's loud. Heavy. The sound of the waves slap-ping against the sand echoes in the frigid air. I switch off the light, dejected.

"I never find them."

Anne nods and reaches for the flashlight. It disappears back into her jacket. She grabs my hand. Takes my glove into her mitten.

"Now can we go?"

Anne walks faster on the way back. Even skips.

"You know," she says, "you're right. I'm glad we came. I can't wait to get under a blanket and watch TV."

"I guess they're not here anymore."

"What?"

"Frostfish...the herring. Probably fished out. Gone. Like everything else."

A patchy cloud floats in front of the moon, causing a flash of sparks to shoot across the sand. The iridescent light dances and wiggles along the beach.

Anne stuffs the plastic bag into her pocket and trudges up the dune to the car.

"Hurry," she calls out.

I walk behind in measured steps, careful to avoid the shimmering spots of light. Weaving around them as if they were frost fish that came just for me.

Life After Death

SHE WAS PETITE and wide-eyed, dressed smartly in bell-bottom jeans and a white sweater. We caught eyes a few times at the party before I finally got the nerve to talk to her. I thought we made a connection, so when she said she was leaving I asked if she wanted to have dinner sometime to continue our conversation. She joked back that she didn't like to eat and talk at the same time. I said that was okay—that we didn't need to say a word to each other if that meant her going out with me. I remember she looked at me, hard, for a few moments, and then stuck her hand out to shake as if making a deal. And I guess that's what we did. We agreed to meet up a few nights later at a Moroccan restaurant that featured belly dancing and *Tagine De Legumes*, a delicious vegetable stew. Her name, by the way, was Sylvia.

We met outside the restaurant and Sylvia reiterated that once we sat down, no words were to be spoken between us. I had not forgotten my promise, but I was surprised she meant to follow through on it. But I was game and found her even more attractive in the yellow paisley dress she wore that night. We sat down, and a waiter gave us menus. It was hard to suppress the urge to explain my enthusiasm for the food, the belly dancing, to showcase how creative I was to pick such a spot to dine. I was dying to impress her but constrained by silence. To compensate, I made a point of being overly polite and precise in my movements, spreading out the napkin like an English butler on my lap, daintily sipping from the water glass, perusing the menu with a thoughtful calm even though I knew what I wanted.

When the waiter returned, I nodded to Sylvia, indicating she should go first. She shook her head and then turned toward the waiter and said: "He'll order for us."

I exhaled, relieved that the no-talk rule did not extend to everyone else. But then I got nervous, not sure what Sylvia would like or not. I decided to go with two *Tagine De Legumes* and, to start, a sampler of appetizers that seemed to touch on every food group. I also ordered a bottle of wine, but she shook her head again and pointed to her water glass. I decided to forgo alcohol as well, and when the waiter left I began to feel uncomfortable with our silence. Sylvia, on the other hand, seemed at ease, alternating between looking around the room, sipping water, and smiling at me.

Then the appetizers came. A server helped the waiter, and the two of them placed dish after dish onto the table, until what lay between Sylvia and I

looked like a culinary minefield. I was happy, however, because Sylvia appeared to enjoy the work of
the waiter and server; her eyes sparkled when they
finished, and she looked over the feast. I used my
hands to indicate she should start. She returned
the gesture, but I held firm, determined to be the
complete gentleman. Finally, she reached out, took
a piece of pita bread, and dipped it in hummus. She
held it up, as if inspecting it, and then consumed
it in one bite. Laughing, but without sound, I mim-
icked her method with the pita and hummus, and
with that ice broken, we dove in until we finished all
the appetizers.

Once the stew arrived, I was no longer nervous
about keeping silent or wanting to impress Sylvia.
Something had passed between us during that ini-
tial frenzy of eating, and not just a shared love of
ground chick peas and lamb skewers. I'd like to
think it was a recognition of kindred spirits, of two
people who would go through with such an odd date.
There was also a connection in our movements, the
way we used our forks and spoons and knives, the
way we wiped our faces with our napkins, the way
we lifted our glasses and drank. If I knew I liked
her at the end of the appetizers, I was falling in love
after the stew.

When the waiter came to ask about dessert, Sylvia
lifted her napkin in surrender. I signaled for the
check. But before it came, a woman emerged from

the back room and strode to the center stage. She was tall and thin, draped in silk, and looking for the world like a genie. She had straight black hair that hung to her waist, and silver slippers adorned her feet. She was the belly dancer. Without music or introduction, she began to move, starting with pronounced circling of her hips, and then progressing to fast gyrations, dizzying in the speed, dazzling in the line. When she finished to loud applause, I saw that Sylvia was crying. Silent tears, of course. But they flowed free and easy down her face. Seeing her cry and being so moved by the dancer, my growing ardor for Sylvia, all and everything I felt at that moment, I cried too. And together we walked away from the table, with me leaving behind cash for the bill plus a larger tip than necessary, arm and arm, weeping without sound, until we got outside. Sylvia spoke first.

"I enjoyed this so much," she said, pulling her arm from mine and wiping at her tears with the back of her right hand. "Too much, I'm afraid."

I didn't hear, or didn't focus, on her last words, so glad to hear she had a good time to think of anything else.

"I'm sorry," she continued, "but I can't go out with you again."

This I heard.

"What?"

"I can't see you anymore."

"But we had a good time. I mean, we didn't even talk, and it was great."

"I know, but that's the problem. I already have feelings for you. If we go out again, and talk, and they deepen ..."

"Yes. What's wrong with that? I have feelings for you already as well."

She nodded her head, as if affirming an interior thought. She was no longer crying.

"That's even more reason to end this now."

"I don't get it." I reached for her arm, but she dodged it. "Help me understand."

She inhaled deep, held it, then exhaled.

"Not tonight. I can meet you tomorrow, for coffee. There's a café one block away. I'll be there at noon if you want to meet me. But it's not a date. You can't think of it as anything but me giving you an explanation."

"Can I talk?" I asked, anger and hurt making me snippy.

"Of course. But I won't change my mind."

"But ..."

My word fell flat on an empty space. She had turned and was walking away. I watched until she was out of sight, and then I walked the other way, back to my apartment and my swirling thoughts.

I got to the café ten minutes before noon. Sylvia wasn't there, but I got a latte and found an empty table, sat down, and stared at my phone until she

43

walked in. She was wearing the same outfit she wore when I first met her, but there was something different in her appearance; she didn't seem as shiny, as precious, but more worn and weary. She sat down and smiled, but it was without sparkle.

"Do you want a coffee?"

She shook her head.

"I'm too tired for caffeine. It will make me jittery when my body wants to shut down. Not a good combination."

I sipped my latte, more to gather my thoughts.

"You have something to tell me?"

"I do."

"I'm listening."

She bit at her lower lip and then released it and blew out her lips before speaking.

"I never should have gone out with you."

"I'm that bad," I blurted out defensively.

She reached over and put her hand on mine.

"No, not at all. I don't mean anything about you. You see ..."

"What is it?"

She pulled back her hand.

"I'm married."

I recoiled, as if punched in the face.

"I know it was wrong to go out with you, but I was so lonely. When you said the thing about not talking, it seemed so strange but in a safe way. Like I wasn't cheating."

"If it's that bad, why don't you just leave your husband? Then you can go out like a normal person."

"I can't."

"Why not? People divorce all the time. He can't make you stay in the marriage."

"No, you see, he left me. Six months ago. He fell in love with someone else and lives with her. But we're not divorced."

"But you're separated," I said. "And he left you. You're not cheating on him by going out with me."

"I know that. But I'm cheating on me. I'm still married, and I still haven't cut that bond, legally or emotionally. It's starting to chip away, fray at the edges, but it's still there. I think going out with you took a big chunk out of it. But it's still in place, and if I keep on with you, I'll start rushing things and feel pulled and prodded toward love."

"Good," I nearly shouted. "Don't you want to know if we have that capacity? I know I do. I like you. I spent a whole night eating dinner with you without saying a word, and I had the best time in my life."

She bit at her lip again.

"Remember when I cried?"

"Of course," I said. "I cried too."

"It wasn't because of the belly dancing, or you, or anything connected to last night."

"So what was it?"

"A poem. Do you know 'Life After Death' by Ted Hughes?"

"No, but it sounds cheery."

She blinked hard at me.

"I'm sorry," I said. "I'm just upset at what you're telling me. What is it about this poem?"

Her face softened.

"My father is a huge poetry fan and loves Sylvia Plath," she said. "I'm named after her. She was married to Ted Hughes. He wrote the poem after she committed suicide. It's about his living with their children after her passing—how she's gone but still there."

She paused, and I gave her time to continue.

"I have the poem printed out, near my bed. I read it often because I feel just like him. Like my husband is still with me, but he's not."

I started to see where she was going. But I was not ready to concede her to her grief, even if that was the path to her healing.

"We don't have to date or be a couple," I said. "We can just hang out as friends. I don't even mind if we don't talk. Just being together is good."

"I told you, I'm not changing my mind. This is right for me, and for you."

"Why don't I feel the same?"

"Because you're not taking the gamble."

"What do you mean?"

"It's like nature, like right now, early spring. Flowers are sprouting, birds are coming back, things are coming alive. But everything is so fragile, and so tenuous. A cold snap, a surprise snow, bad weather can wipe them out, kill their chances to move forward, to live. The ones that come early, be it bud or bird, are taking a risk. If the weather is good, they are first in and thrive and beat their competitors. But if not, then they are doomed, and the ones that come later will succeed. You see, if I go out with you, I'm taking that risk. Do you understand?"

I didn't, and I did. I tried one last time.

"I can wait. Take time and then we can get together again ... when you're ready."

"It doesn't work that way. If I think you're waiting for me, I will want to hurry and get to you. Please, just let it go."

She stood.

"Take care of yourself. And thank you for going out with me and being silent. It means more than you can know."

And she was gone.

The next few days I hurt. I felt I had lost a potential soulmate, a chance for lasting love. I could not eat and could not sleep. I took to taking long walks at night, sometimes nearly to dawn. I even bought a book of poetry by Ted Hughes that had "Life After Death" in it. I read the poem as if it was a glass of wine, sipping the words, taking my time, trying to find the meaning that meant so much to Sylvia. But the only lines that stuck were about wolves, about their mournful howls into and under a falling snow, voices that invite others to accept with them the painful truth about life and death.

I understood. I felt like a wolf, wailing into the
silence, pining for Sylvia and nursing my romantic
wound. One night, it all came together. I had been
walking for hours, and had ventured far from the city
limits, to the edge of a wild preserve and rows of tall
poplars that shaded the forest within. It was a clear
night and cold for spring. But then it got colder, the
wind kicked up, and the sky changed from clear to
gray and then white. Snow began to fall, first light-
ly, but then with spirit, until it was near-blinding
conditions. I thought about what Sylvia had said
about gamblers, and the new buds and early birds
and all the living things jeopardized by a late season storm. It made me connect, finally, to her pain,
to her reasoning, to her logic. I felt like crying, and
I might have, except I lost my breath when a wolf
emerged from the trees and came towards me. I did
not run as it approached. I was not scared. I was
willing to gamble, to take a risk, that it might free
me from my torment. One way or another.

Shanghai Cut

WILLIAM HOLDS his new wife's hand in the darkness, her father's snoring loud from the lone bedroom a floor below.

"You know, he never passed on his skill," she tells him, the hard edges of her accent smoothed over after fifteen years in the States. "The Shanghai Cut."

William opens his eyes. He lifts up from the misshapen air mattress they've endured since her father's visit.

"The what?"

"The Shanghai Cut."

She explains. Her father, a retired barber from Taiwan, learned his trade as a young man in Shanghai, a city reputed to have the best barbers in Asia.

"Shanghai was known for three cuts," she says, making chopping motions with her right hand, her opaque skin slicing a light trail through the air. "Chef, tailor, and barber. You know—cut food, cut cloth, and cut hair."

William's nostrils flare at the imagined smells of stir-fried vegetables, treated leather, talcum powder.

"In Chinese," she adds. "We say that scissors are like two knives together."

The information grabs William's attention, diverting his mind from anxious thoughts of the coming workday.

"What's the Shanghai Cut look like?"

"It's very conservative," she answers. "My father says you must cut right down to the roots, so the hair will stay neat and in place, even in a typhoon."

She pauses, draws a breath, exhales.

"But customers also get a wash, massage, facial, shave, manicure, ear-cleaning. That's part of it, too."

William runs a hand over his bristled scalp. A few days before, he'd gone to a hair salon, a nationwide chain charging thirty-five bucks for a shampoo and cut. A woman in her early twenties with a tattooed neck finished his hair in five minutes, snapping bubble gum the whole time she raked an electric razor over his head.

"I'd never leave your father's chair," he says.

"Oh, his customers loved him. He was famous in Taiwan because he had important clients: celebrities, politicians, businessmen. They never went to any other barber."

William pulls her hand close to his lips. Her fingertips smell of fried fish and dish soap, a product of her dinner duties that night.

"He never passed it on, the Shanghai Cut?"

"No."

"Why?"

"The style isn't popular anymore. Young people don't want to learn something only a few old people want. My father had to apprentice more than three years in Shanghai before he could start his business in Taiwan. Who has that much time and patience nowadays?"

William understands. He thinks of himself at work, busy and distracted, flitting from one task to the next, unable to concentrate long enough to complete any of them.

"I wish he could speak English," he says. "He could teach me."

They grow silent when the snoring downstairs stops, followed by hard coughing. They hear the soft creaking of floorboards, the gentle closing of the bathroom door.

"A Chinese doctor told him his prostate is weak," she whispers. "My father's very worried about it."

They hear the toilet flush, the sound of feet padding back to bed. The snoring resumes after several minutes.

"I mean it," William says. "I'd like to be a barber. Talking to people all day. Getting to know them while I cut their hair. Don't you think it sounds nice?"

His wife doesn't answer. He realizes she's also fallen asleep, puffing out faint breaths from her small lips.

William closes his eyes and drifts into fantasy. He imagines owning an old-fashioned barbershop with gold-plated chairs and white porcelain sinks with smooth ivory handles. He sees smoked-glass mirrors lining the walls and a glistening parquet floor underfoot. A thick parfait glass on a polished marble shelf holds a spray of black plastic combs drowning in green-dyed antiseptic. Next to it is an opened teak carrying case holding scissors and razors, each shined and sharpened to perfection, gleaming atop the blue velvet lining.

As for him, he wears a white cotton smock over a navy dress shirt, its starched collar noosed smartly by a silken tie. His slacks are pleated and made of gray flannel, the cuffs tapering gracefully into a pair of newly buffed, brown loafers. In his lapel sprouts a single red poppy, and his lone jewelry is a sparkling, silver-banded wristwatch that clinks and clacks as he snaps a mahogany-handled whiskbroom across the spotless floor. And when the first customer of the day comes through the door, a debonair gentleman in a somber three-piece suit with matching wingtips, William bows slightly, guides him to the chair with a confident hand, calmly awaiting his request for the Shanghai Cut.

Spin

GAIL'S MOTHER gripped the sides of the recliner as if they were handlebars on a ten-speed.

"Teal's son loves the class," she said. "He says it's a great burn."

"You and Teal talk about great burns?"

"Don't be smart," her mother scolded. "Teal's son met his last girlfriend in the class. A psychologist. They were in love until they broke up."

"What happened?"

"You know professional women. No time. Too busy. Want too much."

Gail did not appreciate the comment. She was forty-one and held a high position at a human resources firm. Many times she had gone on dates with men who seemed to lose interest in her after she spoke about her work or learned about her success.

She crouched her eyebrows with annoyance.

"Spare me. I'm a professional woman and all I want is a man who can walk and talk at the same time."

"You should be more picky. But pick right. Like your father."

"Dad met you where? At a bar?"

"Why so nasty today? I'm trying to help you get burned and meet a man."

Her mother clumsily pushed out of the chair. She straightened up with random snaps from both knees.

"Anyway, I have to get ready."

"Where are you going?"

"The senior center. A nurse is coming to give free cholesterol screenings, and then we're having strawberry shortcake and coffee."

"Sounds nice."

"It passes the time."

Her mother looked hard at Gail.

"Do me one favor and call Teal's son. His number is on the envelope on the table. His name is Ryan. I'd try to match you, but Teal said he's not interested in settling down. He's a playboy. But maybe you'll meet someone else. Keep your eyes open. Miracles do happen."

Gail thought for a moment to chastise her mother for the subtle put-down, but decided it best to let the matter drop, hoping, in some way, that she was right.

Ryan sounded like a long-time smoker, his voice phlegmy, deep, and raspy. Gail figured he was sitting at the kitchen table as they spoke, phone in one hand, cigarette in the other, ashes dripping on a

Formica table, the tips of his fingers yellow-stained, the whole place smelling stale, acrid, cancerous.

"My mom said you might call. Glad to hear from you. Excuse me a second."

Gail waited as Ryan ripped out a series of coughs.

"Swallowed wrong," he finally said.

"I can call back."

"I'm fine. Anyway, class is 7:00 p.m. on Thursdays. The teacher is good. Her name is Pauline. She plays mostly house music. Most people are in their late thirties, early forties. Pretty balanced."

Ryan coughed again. Gail wondered how he could ever get through a class. She imagined him clutching his chest over the bike, his body shaking in spasms, a cigarette pack rolled under his t-shirt.

"Is the class hard?" she asked. "I haven't worked out in a while. "

"You'll be fine," Ryan half-choked in response. "My mother says you have a nice shape. You shouldn't have a problem."

Gail blushed.

"Hello."

"Uh, yeah. Sorry. Does it cost anything?"

"Are you a member of the YMCA?"

"No."

"Then it's ten dollars. But I have a guest pass you can use. If you want to come and try it out, I'll put your name at the desk."

"Okay," Gail said, "thanks."

"No problem," Ryan said, slipping into another coughing jag.

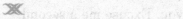

Ryan didn't smell like cigarette smoke. He smelled like cigarette smoke buried in aftershave. He was short and thin with straggly gray hair and close-set green eyes that stared down his long nose. His face was shiny and newly shorn.

"A few of us usually go for a fruit smoothie after class," he said. "You should join us. It's a good way to replenish."

Gail searched the room for a bike in the back, out of sight. She was already regretting coming to the class.

"Oh, I probably can't," she said. "I have some work to do tonight."

"Here, take the bike next to me." Ryan said, coughing into his palm. "You have water. Good. Now strap in and warm up a bit. But go easy today. Maybe I'm giving you too much advice. Just have fun."

Gail climbed on the bike, adjusted the seat, and began peddling in slow arcs. She hadn't exercised much since she broke up with Gavin, her last serious relationship. Gavin was an advertising salesman who played in a blues band. They used to ride together in a local park on the weekends. But that was nearly five years ago.

People streamed into the room amid happy chatter and puffed and pulled and arranged themselves on the bikes. Gail's eyes darted around the room—at the hands of the men and the bodies of the women. All the ladies looked younger and in better shape than her; all the men had wedding rings, except Ryan.

Pauline, the instructor, walked in and clapped her hands twice. She was round as a beach ball and wore a one-piece pink Lycra sweat suit. Her hair was bound up in a bun and she had heavy black eyeliner and purple lipstick.

"Anyone new to the class?" she asked.

Ryan pointed at Gail.

"Over here."

Gail blushed and lowered her head. When she looked up, Pauline was standing beside her bike, gripping the handlebars.

"Know how to ride a bike?"

"Yes."

"This is the same, but you aren't going anywhere. You can still get hurt, though. People make that mistake all the time. They think because the bike isn't moving they don't have to be safe. They get on wrong. Or get off wrong. And break their ankles. Twist their knees. Wrench their backs. Do you know how to stop fast?"

Gail shook her head.

Pauline pointed at the pedals.

"Pull up on that knob below the handlebars. Tighten those straps up. And raise the seat a little. Are you more comfortable?"

"I think so," Gail said.

"Don't worry," Pauline said. "It'll be over in an hour."

Gail's mother was in bed. She looked whiter than the painted walls in her apartment.

"How do you feel?"

"Horrible. I was throwing up all night."

Gail pulled open the blinds. It was a sunny morning. No clouds. A blue sky. She placed her palm flat against the windowpane. The glass was still cool but warming in the morning light.

"You probably ate too much cake."

"Ah. I only had a little. The strawberries weren't much, anyway." Her mother raised her right hand out of the sheets and pinched her ring and index fingers together. "Tiny. Like peanuts."

"Does your stomach still hurt?"

"Nothing left in it to hurt. I just feel tired. I'm an old lady. What do you expect?"

Gail went into the bathroom, turned on the faucet, rinsed and then filled a dusty glass sitting on the sink. Next to her, rows of pill bottles filled a portable tray. Inside the bathtub was a special railing so her mother could lower and raise herself into the water.

She had always taken baths. Never showers. It was the best memory of Gail's childhood. The sound of her mother running a bath as Gail lay in bed. The soft gurgle floating through the wall. The light splashing. Her mother humming. Then, always later, a kiss good night. Her mother's hair wrapped in a towel. Her body in a terry cloth bathrobe. Her face warm and clean and smelling like soap. Clean and safe and warm. She hadn't felt that in a long time.

Gail came back into the room and placed the glass on her mother's night table.

"Drink that when you get a chance," she said. "You're probably dehydrated."

"Teal told me you went to the bicycle thing."

"Spin class."

"Well?"

"It was okay."

"Did you get burned?"

"I sweated like a pig."

"How did you like Ryan?"

"He's fine. Friendly."

Her mother struggled for the water and pressed the glass to her lips. She swallowed in sips and then rested it back on the table.

"A playboy. That's what Teal says. Says he has women calling him all the time. A real ladies' man."

"Yeah," Gail said. "I can see that."

"You're coming to class tonight, right?"

Gail was at work. She stared at a spreadsheet on her computer screen, wondering how she would make it to the end of the day without falling asleep. She had Ryan on the speaker, his voice reverberating in her little cubicle. She heard her boss's voice coming near, snatched the phone, and held it to her ear.

"I'm a little tired."

"I'm beat too," Ryan said. "I went out last night after work. Stayed way too late." He coughed three times, each deeper and longer than the next. "Maybe I'm getting too old for this stuff."

"What stuff?"

"Partying. I'm forty-four. I should be married and tucking in kids by now."

Her cell phone buzzed. It was her mother.

"Okay," she suddenly said to Ryan. "I'll go to Spin tonight."

"Great. Why don't …"

"Sorry," she interrupted him, reaching over to click off the speaker. "I have to take another call."

Gail's legs burned. They were standing up for two counts, sitting for two. Up and down. Up and down. The song was ending. Pauline yelled out. "Finish strong. Don't give up." Up and down. Up and down.

Her sweat poured out in a straight line under the bike. She focused on it. Watched it pool and roll towards Ryan's bike. "Everyone sit back down. Take the tension off. Coast. Flush out your legs. Drink some water."

Gail continued to ride hard. The burn seared. She gritted her teeth.

"Everyone slow down. Bring your bike to a stop."

Ryan caught Pauline's eye and they both looked over at Gail.

"Hey," he said, "we're done."

"Sorry," Gail said. She slowed her legs and then got off the bike and joined the class in stretching. Coated in sweat, Ryan handed her a towel.

"I always bring an extra," he said.

"Thanks."

"Hey," he coughed. "I heard your mother wasn't feeling well, how is she?"

Gail scrunched her eyebrows.

"Better, I hope. She called me right after I spoke with you."

Ryan removed his headband and pushed back his hair. "Yeah. These old ladies are tough. They don't sit around feeling sorry for themselves. They're something. My mother can hardly see three feet in front of her, but she has an opinion about any woman I date. She said my last girlfriend was too busty. Can you believe that? Cracked me up."

Gail nodded. She thought about her mother. Lying in bed. The pill tray in the bathroom. The railing in the bathtub.

"I tell you. They get around. Next week they are going on a bus trip to a casino and then to see a concert. I think Tony Bennett. They have a better social life than I do." He coughed hard. "But they stick together. My mom. Your mom. The other ladies. They're like a gang. They look out for each other."

Gail smiled. The room was empty except for Pauline, who gathered up her microphone headset and cassettes. The sweat began to chill on her skin.

Ryan put his hand on her shoulder.

"Would you like to come with us tonight?" he asked. "To get a shake."

"No, I can't," she said, moving away from his touch. "I'm going to see my mother. See how she is."

Ryan's eyes dropped and he stifled a cough with a fist.

"That's nice. I should see my mother more."

"But maybe next time," Gail said. "I mean, getting a shake."

"Sure," Ryan returned. "Whatever you decide."

In the locker room, Gail showered quickly, changed, and was out the door when she ran into Ryan and a few others from the class mingling in front of the building.

"Take care," Ryan said. "Hope your mom is feeling better."

Gail smiled and waved. "Thanks."

She began walking away from the group and pulled out her cell to check messages. There was one. It was from her mother. She was at the hospital. Something had happened to Teal. Gail listened until the end and then began to walk to where Ryan was still talking with the group. He saw her eyes and stopped. And then he began walking toward her.

Burned Out

It was freezing outside, and I was smoking the cold while I waited for the door to the trailer to open. I took an imaginary drag from my fingers and blew out what I hoped to be a smoke ring, but it came out a mushroom cap. I was about to give it another go when Curry stuck his head out a window at the far end of the trailer.

"It's open, what are you waiting for?"

"I don't walk into people's homes uninvited," I answered. "It's how you get shot."

"Funny. Got wood?"

"In the car. I was seeing if you were alone first."

"What time is it?"

"Around three."

"I'm alone. Get the piece and haul ass before someone beats you to it."

I went to the car, got the log, and returned to the trailer. This time I walked in without knocking. I warmed instantly and removed my hat and coat and gloves. Curry was still at the window but pulled his head in. He shut it and plopped down in a beach chair festooned with green cushions. Next to him was a compact wood-burning stove, and inside more ember than fire.

"Give me your offering."

I passed him the log. He lifted it to his eyes and smiled.

"Birch. My favorite. You can stay."

I took the beach chair across from him and watched as he opened the stove and tossed in the log. He kicked the hatch door closed and relaxed in the chair.

"What's up?"

I listened to the snap and crackle of a fire happy to have new fuel to live on.

"I'm reading again."

"I didn't know you stopped."

"I told you last time."

"That was a few logs ago."

I guess this is a good time to let you know more about Curry. To start, despite living in a trailer on a bleak lot in a bleak area outside Boston, he has money, lots of it. He made a pile as a commercial lobsterman, which is not an easy thing to do if your only source of income is lobsters. And before you go and presume that Curry's wealth came from the trafficking of a different product altogether, I will tell you he became rich on the up and up, not only in a manner that was lawful, but which owed itself fully to the law. You see, Curry sued the government of

Massachusetts, specifically the Marine Patrol, for a series of unwarranted stops and searches of his boat in the pursuit of his profession. It was a period of regular harassment causing him to experience acute anxiety, deep depression, and a significant loss of income which, according to his lawyer, came to about five million dollars in compensation.

Now you might think Curry's claim far-fetched and excessive, and ordinarily you might be right. But the reality is that during the time they stopped his boat for no good reason, well, I'll get to the no-good reason in a bit, Curry did endure acute anxiety, deep depression, and a significant loss of income. The only problem was that Curry had been experiencing all this for years, long before the lobster season in question. The jury, however, did not take this into account given two key pieces of evidence: a naked photo of a comely, mature woman, which, on the back, "Never forget I love you. B." was handwritten. And a second photo, the entire frame consisting of a woman's fist with middle finger raised, and on the back handwritten, in the same pen as the other: "Never forget I love you. B."

B., it turned out, was short for Bernadette, who, coincidently, was a member of the Boston Harbor Marine Patrol. She admitted under oath that not only did she harass Curry, but she would do it again if given the chance.

Curry got his money. He sold his boat, bought the trailer, and, borrowing from FDR's radio announcements to an anxious nation during World War II, began his own "fireside chats" as a way of moving on.

"How many are there now?"

Curry scrunched his face in concentration. When he released the muscles his skin held the wrinkles a moment before realizing they were free to spread out and hide.

"About ten regulars," he said. "And another ten who come now and then."

I nodded, impressed.

"What about today?"

"You're the fourth."

"My favorite number."

"Mine's five," he said, smiling.

"I heard."

The fire started to hiss.

"Want to know what I'm reading?" I asked, breaking the silence.

"If you want to tell me."

"*A Burnt-Out Case.*"

"Never heard of it."

"It's by Graham Greene."

Curry shrugged his shoulders.

"He's British."

"That's supposed to mean something?"

This time, I shrugged my shoulders.

"I don't read much anymore," Curry said after a few more pops and snaps from the fire. "Too busy talking, I suppose."

"You're done working for good?"

He closed his eyes a moment, making me think I asked him a difficult question which he was giving much thought. But when he opened them and spoke, I realized it was not my query that distracted him, but something else.

"Do you remember Captain Al? He runs a boat, moored almost directly across from where I used to be in the harbor."

I thought a moment. I had met Curry at the wharf, the summer before my final year of college, when I was running lobsters from the boats to a few restaurants in town. "Sort of. Tall guy?"

"That's the one. He's six-foot-five, easy."

"What about him?"

"He came by about a week ago. He heard what I was up to and brought a piece of his boat to burn. A nice chunk of cedar planking from the hatch."

"Why'd he do that?"

"Because he's getting divorced and the boat is in his wife's name; meaning she gets it. He told me was going to sink it, but the damn thing is stuck frozen in the ice right now, so he figures he'll just gut it instead and let her have the husk."

"Seems petty ... and possibly criminal."

"That's Captain Al. He's not nice, but the cedar burned beautifully and smelled nice."

"You don't inform on companions as long as their wood is good?"

"Who am I to judge on anyone else?"

Curry eyed the stove. My birch was half gone and slimming fast.

"How's things with your wife?"

I thought a moment before answering.

"Good. But she misses home."

"Where's that again?"

"Near Tampa. On the Gulf Coast."

"Is that a problem?"

"You mean, would she rather be on a warm beach than freezing up here?"

Curry looked at me with the same expression as he did my log. I raised my hand to acknowledge my sarcasm wasn't lost on him.

"No, it's not a problem with us. We're not fighting and we laugh a lot. I just worry I should be taking the hint and moving us down there."

"What about work? You like your job, right?"

"I like the pay. How do you think I can afford birch?"

Curry saw my joke for what it was: I wanted to get off the subject. Gratefully, he let me.

"If you don't mind, I got a story to share. But I warn you: it will finish your log."

I nodded, somewhat relieved. "Please. I'm tired of hearing my own voice."

"It's about Captain Al. I didn't tell you why he's getting divorced. Want to guess?"

"Since she's getting his boat and all, I'd say he cheated on her."

"Close, in that he cheated, but it was not with a woman ... or a man. It was with an idea."

I made a face.

"I know," Curry said, "it sounds odd, but it's what he told me. He said he was unfaithful because he had an idea that his wife might be better off without him as a husband. That didn't mean he wanted to leave her or end up divorced. And he also was not in the mind to think she should be with someone else or alone. His idea was that he would stay with her, but as a friend and a lover, not as a legally wed husband. He figured if his wife saw him as something other than a husband, it would remind her of what he was before he was her husband. It would be reinvigorating for her, awaken old memories, desires, fears, insecurities, and lust. He thought it was a rebellious and sexy idea."

There was a loud snap from the oven, and I saw my log, what was left of it, split into two parts, each the size of a flattened baseball.

"But she didn't. His wife heard him out one night, didn't see any merit in the idea, certainly

71

didn't consider it sexy, and basically withdrew into a stew for months until ..."

Curry paused, watching the fire burning itself out.

"What?"

"Until she met me. Captain Al's wife was in the Marine Patrol."

"His wife is Bernadette?"

"Bingo. The infamous B. We met and things got complicated."

"And you got rich."

"I guess you can say that."

I made another face, but this time I spoke before Curry could answer the gesture. "And Captain Al came to see you. I mean, didn't you think he might bean you with the cedar rather than give it up as a gift?"

Curry shrugged. "It's the rule I made to myself: if someone comes with an offering of wood for my fire, I let them in to talk."

"You took a risk."

"More like I've given up worrying what is right or wrong, what is risky or isn't risky. I just live by a simple rule and let the chips fall as they will."

"Ash, you mean."

"Touché."

I looked at the stove. There was just a lick of flame on two small cups of embers.

"Looks like my time is up?"

Curry nodded.

"It's been good."

"Yeah."

I stood, my legs a little tight from sitting.

"You know," I said. "You should read that book I was talking about: *A Burnt-Out Case*. It's a little bit like the story you told me."

"Captain Al's idea?"

"More like you in this trailer."

"How so?"

"You'll have to read it for yourself. What do you say?"

Curry bit at his lip.

"Okay. Bring it with you next time. But one condition."

"What's that?"

"I get to burn it after."

"Deal."

I bundled up and went out the door. Coming toward me, toward the trailer, was a woman wearing a full-body parka. In her hand was a large wooden baseball bat. It was an interesting item to offer to Curry's fire. But I gave it no more thought as we passed.

Untuckit 35

JASON WAS SINGLE, in his mid-thirties, had recently moved to a new town, and worked out of his apartment as a freelance graphic designer. Most of his close friends were drifting away due to marriages and relationships, children being born and raised, and escalating job pressures. He was not particularly tight with his family.

As a result of this confluence of non-connection, Jason was lonely. When he heard a nearby community center hosted a "Saturday Night Social" each week, he summoned his courage, shoved aside his natural shyness, bought some new denim jeans and a matching Untuckit shirt to wear, and went to the party.

The community center was a large, rectangular building. The exterior walls were painted dark blue, while the entrance doors were a shade lighter. Once he pushed through them, a woman around his age greeted him.

She looked him over before speaking.

"Is that an Untuckit shirt?"

Jason blushed.

"Yes. I just bought it."

"Nice. Looks natural. Like you meant to have it hang over your belt."

"I guess that's the concept."

"I suppose you're right. Are you here for the social?"

Jason nodded.

"Good. Let's get you started."

Jason noticed she held a clipboard. She snatched a pen from behind her ear and started asking him questions in rapid-fire fashion.

"Name. Last first."

He gave it.

"Job."

He told her.

"Relationship status?"

"Excuse me."

"Single? Dating? Married? Divorced?"

"Why do you need to know that?"

She lowered her clipboard. "You don't have to tell me if you don't want to. But you can only come in if you answer all the questions. That's our policy."

Jason looked over her shoulder. There was one more set of doors past the lobby. Inside, he saw, was packed with people.

"Single."

"Dating?"

"Not right now."

"Age?"

"Thirty-five."

"Do you have a preferred nickname? If you don't, we can assign one."

"I don't understand."

"You have to go by a nickname once inside. That's policy as well."

"Some people call me Will."

"I'm afraid that's too close to your real name. And it's only four letters. We require a nickname that's over six letters. Also, it's best if you include either a number or a grammar mark, like an exclamation point.

"You're kidding!"

She started to look frustrated. "I'm going to go ahead and give you one." She did a fast scan of her clipboard. "How does 'Untuckit 35' sound?"

"Weird."

"But can you live with it?

"I guess."

"Perfect. Once inside, anyone asks you, that's your name."

"We're done?"

She didn't answer, already looking past him and to a couple coming through the doors. He took it as a cue to move on and go inside.

Jason was surprised by how loud it was, but also how disconnected the noise was from all the disparate talking going on. The space was open and without walls, but people settled more or less in defined groups. In the larger groups, he noticed, one person stood in the middle, encircled by others, sometimes two to three rows deep.

He weaved through the room, listening and seeing where he might make an introduction or find an opening to join. Finally, he came upon a group of five people—two women and three men—who seemed more approachable.

"Hello," he said. "Mind if I join?"

"Of course you can," said one of the women, stepping out of the group to meet him. "What's your name?"

Jason remembered the policy. "Untuckit 35."

"Ah ... your shirt," she returned with a wink. "And I bet your age. Easy to figure out."

"It was assigned to me."

She paused for a moment. "Just to let you know, we're only talking about birds of prey this evening."

"Excuse me?"

She held her arms out to the side like airplane wings and moved her upper body about as if soaring.

"You know, hawks, eagles, falcons. That's our connecting conversation."

She lowered her arms and came to a staggered stillness. "We were just discussing the Northern Shrike. Its nickname is the 'Butcher Bird' because it impales its catch on spiky plants or barbered wire fences."

Jason resisted the urge to grimace. "I'm sorry," he said. "I don't really know much about birds, except that I hate pigeons."

She eyed him a moment, as if considering a question, and then nodded before speaking. "I bet there's an anti-pigeon talk going on somewhere in the room. Just keep looking. It does take all kinds."

She returned to her group, and Jason, starting to feel uncomfortable, continued on. But he didn't have any more success in meeting people or making friends. In addition to most groups having set criteria for discussion that excluded him, the few people he did manage to talk to seemed more intent to just tell him things, ticking off, as if reading a recording, what they liked to do, or what they had done, places they'd visited, and where they would like to visit. One gentleman even provided a detailed description of his week's meals, a daily breakdown of breakfast, lunch and dinner, including caloric content and flavor gradients.

It made Jason dizzy and disoriented and even more detached. A few times, he felt defensive, as several individuals, standing on the fringes of a group, shouted out random accusations, implying the guilt of all for something that grieved them. Some even held up elaborately-designed posters, giving images to their exhortations, or played music from portable boom boxes to dramatize the message.

Finally, his nerves frayed, Jason made a hasty exit.

The woman greeter half-shouted to him as he hustled through the lobby.

"I hope you had a good time, Untuckit 35? Please come again."

He pushed through the last set of doors and was outside.

It was a pleasant, clear night, and the moon was full. It gave enough light for him to find a park bench in a pocket park a few blocks away. He sat and tried to calm his breathing. After a few moments, an elderly man, aided by a cane, strolled by with his dog on a leash.

He eyed Jason and smiled.

"Do you mind if I sit down with you? We always take our break here."

Jason slid over to one side.

"Sure."

The old man sat with a pleased grunt. The dog, a poodle variety, settled near his feet.

"Nice evening. But they say it's going to rain later. We could use it. The plants, that is. You garden?"

Jason was surprised by the question.

"No, I mean. I live in an apartment."

"You have a balcony?"

"Yes, but it's tiny."

"That's room enough. If you get some sun, put some herbs in a planter. Or tomatoes or peppers in a few pots. It's fun to watch them grow, and vegetables always taste better when you pick them yourself. Anyway, that's one of my hobbies. Gardening."

"Sounds nice."

"It keeps me occupied. That and walking my friend here."

They were silent a moment.

"Do you have any hobbies?" the old man broke the quiet. "If you don't mind me asking."

Jason lowered his head. "Probably not enough. I mean, I should get some."

"What do you like to do?"

"Normal things, I suppose."

"Like what? I'm sorry to pry, but I enjoy learning about people. It's another hobby, I imagine. Or maybe I'm just lonely."

Jason's throat suddenly constricted and his eyes watered. He felt embarrassed by the surge of emotion and wiped away the forming tears with the back of his hand. "I'm sorry," he finally said, regaining his composure. "But I'm afraid you'll find that I'm not that interesting."

The old man reached over and playfully tapped Jason's shoe with the end of his cane.

"Here's a secret," he said. "None of us are. But the key is to be *interested*. Not interesting."

He stood up from the bench.

"Anyway, time for us to keep going. We circle the park four times before calling it quits. Takes us an hour exactly. Thanks again for sharing the bench. And for the talk."

"I didn't say much."

"I enjoyed it all the same."

The old man cajoled the dog to stand up and together, they started to move away.

Jason took in a breath and called out to him.

"Do you mind if I join you? I think a walk would be good for me."

The old man turned and smiled. "That would be nice. But I warn you, we move slow."

"That's fine. I'm in no hurry."

As they walked around the park, they talked and shared stories, laughed and connected on many points. Without much effort, or any plan, they started a friendship. And Jason, for the first time in a long time, did not feel lonely.

Schmear Campaign

BOBBY AND MATTHEW, both in their early thirties, worked together at a company that sold software products. While not close friends, they were close colleagues between being on the same marketing team, sitting near each other in the office, and having similar roles in the business.

Both were well-liked within the company and good at their jobs, but Bobby had a slight edge when it came to popularity and performance. Matthew did not think this unjust or unfair. Bobby was smart and a hard worker, helpful around the office, always respectful, and good-humored. He was also physically attractive, tall and slim, with wide, muscled shoulders and the tapered waistline of a swimmer. The suits he wore to work were always snappy and well cut for his angular frame. And his hair, thick and brown, never seemed out of place.

Matthew, on the other hand, was insecure about his looks, particularly the growing paunch around his middle, and a thick neck that made it difficult to fasten the top button of a collared shirt. His hair also troubled him. He kept it long enough in college to rock the occasional "man-bun." But since graduation it had thinned, requiring creative combing to achieve full skull coverage. It made him self-conscious, and when not at work, he usually wore a baseball cap, indoors or outdoors.

Personality-wise, Matthew also felt that he was lacking. He was intelligent, but he wished he was wittier, struggling to keep up with people who were quick with a quip or had perfect timing when telling a joke. He considered himself more a plodder when it came to conversation, and he always worried, particularly at dinner parties or events, that he would bore them with his inability to engage in lively talk when he was seated next to someone he did not know well.

Despite all this, Matthew did not envy Bobby. If anything, he admired him, perhaps too much, thinking it incredulous that his colleague had no flaws. The idea made him even more aware of his own perceived failings, and, whenever he noticed something positive about Bobby, be it a well-coordinated shirt and tie, or a laugh-producing remark made in a staff meeting, he reflexively reminded himself that he held no such gifts.

But as time progressed, and the two men continued on with the company, Matthew's attention to all that was great about Bobby edged toward obsession. Perhaps it coincided with forward movement in Bobby's life: he got engaged while Matthew remained single; he got promoted, Matthew did not; he bought a house, Matthew continued to rent.

Still, Matthew did not feel jealous of Bobby, only more and more exasperated that nothing was wrong with him. The notion began to consume him, thinking it unnatural for a person not to have any weaknesses. Finally, when it got to the point he had trouble being around Bobby, he knew he had to address the issue.

And so Matthew committed himself to discovering an imperfection in Bobby, something that would make him feel better about his own imperfections. But no matter how hard he tried to notice something untoward about Bobby, he couldn't. Days and weeks went by, months, and nothing. He even began to toy with the paranoid thought that Bobby was an alien in human disguise, a god placed among mortals.

At the end of his tether, and legitimately concerned he was sliding toward psychosis, Matthew prayed for a miracle. And it happened. During a conference call one morning, he and Bobby and the rest of the team sat at a long table listening to a squawk box and helping themselves to a tray of breakfast goodies. Matthew watched as Bobby selected an everything bagel. Just as Matthew was going to pick out a donut from the tray, he stopped, his hand frozen in the air, his eyes riveted on Bobby's tie, which, lovely as ever, now held a dollop of cream cheese.

Clearly, Bobby had not noticed the spill, as he kept eating, listening, and later discussing the call with the others with the offending schmear in full view. Matthew was not sure others in the room saw what he saw, or felt what he felt, which, basically, was a release from an enormous burden. He felt free and confident and in control for the first time in a long time. And also grateful to Bobby for making possible this seismic change within him by soiling his tie.

After the meeting, Matthew trailed Bobby to his desk.

"Hey," he said, "you got a little something on your tie."

Bobby sat in his chair and looked down.

"Aw man, why didn't anyone tell me?"

Matthew shrugged, relishing the role of being the helper.

"You know how everyone is—just concerned with themselves." Bobby took a tissue and wiped away the schmear. "I'm such a klutz. I spill something on me all the time. My dry-cleaning bills are crazy."

"Really?"

"My fiancée says I should wear a bib when I eat."

"I never would have guessed."

"C'mon," Bobby said, pulling out a folder. "You see me every day. You must know what a mess I am. But hey, that's what makes us human, right?"

Matthew went back to his own desk and pulled out his own file to work on. But he had trouble concentrating, his emotions falling, wondering why it was so easy for Bobby to be humble, to be so self-assured and open about his failings. It was just another way, Matthew thought, before taking a bite of the donut he brought back to his desk, in which Bobby was perfect.

If only he could be more like that.

Imaginary Friend

I SAT IN A quiet corner of a quiet café on a quiet evening when Steven joined me. I already had finished half of my coffee and fretted away on my phone when he sat down and cleared his throat, twice, an indication he had something important to say or was struggling with a mild form of bronchitis.

"You need an imaginary friend."

"Excuse me?"

"An imaginary friend," he repeated. "You need one."

I shook my head and returned to my phone.

"Don't you want to know why?"

"Do I have a choice?" I half-mumbled as I punched away on the keys.

"Of course. You know I'm not demanding that way."

I could have disagreed. But in truth, despite my seeming indifference, I was intrigued. And also drained from checking my Twitter feed. I put the phone away, finished my coffee, and tried out my best smile.

"You got my full attention. Tell me why."

My encouragement clearly bolstered Steven. He shot me his own smile, much cleaner and more realistic than mine. "Because you're at a crisis point in your life. You're reliant on social media to affirm your self-value, and the only thing it's affirming is that you're not valuable. You also watch too much television, carry a stash of powdered donuts in your backpack, and you lied about your age the other day to get a senior citizen discount for popcorn at the movie theater. You need help."

"In the form of an imaginary friend?"

"Sure. You're a literary man. Remember what Edgar Allan Poe wrote: 'They who dream by day are cognizant of many things which escape those who dream only by night.'"

"Kudos for quoting Poe, but I don't see how it relates."

"Precisely. You have trouble relating. It's one of the three main reasons kids create imaginary friends: to have someone in their life they can better relate to—someone who 'gets' them, who won't hurt their feelings or reject them."

I was becoming uncomfortable with the talk and snapped back.

"Are you done?"

"If you're feeling defensive, then I must be over the target."

I resisted the urge to pull out my phone and calmed my voice.

"Okay. What're the other reasons? You said there were three."

"It's just what I've read in a psychology journal, but imaginary friends can also help children feel more competent. Say a youngster is always reprimanded by a parent for not tying their shoelaces. They can project this discipline onto a make-believe pal, reminding them to tie *their* laces. In their minds, they become the competent adult."

"You read this in a psychology journal?"

"Maybe it was *The New York Times*. Anyway, the other reason is autonomy. A child can use an imaginary friend to gain a greater sense of control. A classic example is bedtime. Say a child wants to inch out a few more minutes before lights-out. They can use as an excuse that they are waiting for their imaginary friend to finish brushing their teeth. Or their friend can't fall asleep without having a story read to them. That kind of thing."

"All well and good for a child," I said. "But I'm more old than young, remember? And with my energy bills, no one has to tell me to turn off the lights."

"Granted. But be honest. You feel more and more lost each day. I bet you don't understand half of the cultural references made on Twitter. And you don't even have an Instagram account. How can you say with a straight face you wouldn't be happier conjuring up a friend who has the same trouble relating to modern life as you do."

"I'm happy enough. I've plenty of friends who don't get what I don't get."

"But what about competence? It might feel nice to give advice to someone who has no choice but to take it."

"That sounds controlling."

"Think of it more as reclaiming autonomy. Just because you're an adult don't think your emotional needs are less than when you were a child. You're more mature and you have more experience, but you also have more responsibilities and pressure. It's a tough world, and there's nothing wrong with making it easier. And it costs nothing. You don't have to buy an imaginary friend a birthday gift, or drive them to the airport, or do whatever you don't want to do with them. You're the creator of the relationship. You're in charge. Doesn't that sound perfect?"

"It's a little odd, though."

"What is?"

"Having an imaginary friend at my age. Won't people think I'm strange or imbalanced?"

"Let them think what they want. You don't seem to care about other things, like wearing compression socks as winter leggings."

"Good point. Still …"

A café worker shouted they were closing. I hadn't realized the time, and I grabbed my phone to check for messages. But Steven's words resounded in my head, and I stopped searching and looked up to tell

him I would give the idea of an imaginary friend serious consideration. But he was gone, vanished into
the proverbial thin air, leaving me alone with my
thoughts, which, perhaps, were more than enough
to get me through the moment.

Whale

JOSÉ PEDDLES fast on a beat-up ten-speed. He glides over a concrete walking path that winds through a treeless park, its grass trampled, brittle and yellow. He comes to the river's edge and stops the bike. He looks across the water, to the gaping hole in the New York City skyline, the two tall buildings that once filled the space removed like excised molars. He remembers the day they were extracted, the phone call from his girlfriend, her last words engulfed in fear.

A flash of movement in the river catches his eye. He stares as the water begins to roil and swirl: something large rises from the depths. In fact, it's gigantic, long and straight, brown, thick, and hissing. It breaks free from the water and hangs in the early evening air, defying gravity, owning the space. Then it crashes back into the river. It stuns José into excitement. He feels alive and scared. He bikes even faster on the way home.

✕

"It was a whale."

Reggie ignores José. He grabs a Snickers from the freezer, fondles it, then sticks it back in. "Not cold enough," he says, disappointed.

He and José share a two-bedroom apartment in Jersey City. They both commute to Manhattan for work: Reggie to teach English to sixth graders, José to tend bar in the West Village. They met at a bereavement group. José was mourning the loss of his girlfriend, Reggie his boyfriend. They moved in together not long after.

"I'm telling you, it was a whale. In the Hudson River."

Reggie brushes by. The kitchen is long and narrow. The apartment is long and narrow. It's a railroad. The kitchen is in the middle. The bathroom is next to the kitchen. Reggie's room is on one end, closest to the bathroom. José's room is on the other end, closest to the kitchen.

"It wasn't a whale."

"Then what was it?" José holds his hands up and apart. "It was a fish, and it was huge."

He follows Reggie into his room. There's a thick leather couch against a wall, directly under a window that looks onto the street. A waterbed adorned with a blue velvet comforter rests against the other wall. A La-Z-Boy sits in between, in front of a wide-screen television. The apartment is on the second floor of a three-story brownstone. José's room is nicer than Reggie's. It's bigger, and the window provides views of a pocket park softened by the glow of streetlights.

Reggie plops into the La-Z-Boy and grabs the remote. He switches on the television. José walks and stands in front. Reggie clicks through him.

"Move."

José squirms, as if rays from the remote are stinging him.

"I swear on my mother's life, I saw a whale."

"You hate your mother."

"Why would I lie?"

"Because you are delusional and in need of attention. You're like my students."

"I'm not lying," José says, raising his voice.

"Okay, I believe you. Now move."

José sets his jaw. "A whale," he says defiantly. I saw it and you didn't."

"Whatever," Reggie flips his hand. "Go get me a Snickers."

José does not sleep well. He wakes early in the morning and shuffles to the kitchen for a glass of water.

Reggie is up, dressed for work, munching on a Twix bar. "What time you go in today?" he asks.

"What day is it?" José responds groggily.

"Monday."

"I'm off."

Reggie swallows the rest of the Twix and rubs his hands together, flicking bits of chocolate and crumbs on the hardwood floor. "Then you can do errands. I left envelopes for the electric and phone bills on the table. Get some stamps and mail them. Plus, pick up some toilet paper. We're down to one roll."

José raises his hand to his forehead in mock salute.

"And I need you to go pick up my DVD player. I already paid for the repair."

"Where's the shop?"

"Right near the park, next to the river."

José rubs hard under his eyes, the force whitening his olive-brown skin. It's his father's color. His mother being white as a ghost, a red-haired Irish woman. José has her eyes, though. Ice blue. Everything else is his dad's.

"What are you teaching today?"

"Still exploring the wonderful world of *Johnny Tremain*," Reggie answers with sarcasm. "Today we read the part where Johnny's hand gets mangled together like a crab by molten silver. I doubt they'll get the metaphor—that America, before the Revolution, is like Johnny's hand: enslaved, crippled, smothered by British rule."

José stops rubbing his eyes and smiles.

"I thought the wounded hand was a punishment for masturbatory fantasies."

"You would think that."

"Makes more sense," José continues. "All writing is sexually based. Whoever wrote *Johnny Tremain* was more interested in whacking off than the American Revolution."

"That's all you're interested in." Reggie frowns. "If you want to keep your hand, mail the letters, buy the toilet paper, and get the DVD."

José looks at his right hand and cups it together. Then opens it and reaches for a glass to fill with water and quench his thirst.

"We're closed. Come back in an hour."

José shields his eyes from the overhead sun and peers into the glass door separating him from a small, oily man with blood-red eyes. It's pitch dark in the store, with no windows other than the door that faces into an alley.

"I need to pick up a DVD player. It's supposed to be ready. Reggie Reynolds."

The man is spectral, wafting in and out of the scant light.

"I don't care. Come back later. One hour."

José looks at his watch. It's noon. He decides to get lunch while he waits. He picks up an egg salad on rye and a Diet Coke and goes a few blocks to a small park that juts out into the river. It's newly built, a landfill, and has a gazebo at the end and several stations for fishermen. He finds a seat on a bench next to an old man wearing a felt fedora and gray linen suit. He eats his lunch in silence and then leans his head back to take in some sun.

"Nice day."

José turns to the old man. "Yes, it is."

"But it might storm later."

José peers up at the sky. "I don't see a cloud anywhere."

"Don't matter," the old man says with a knowing laugh. "When storms come, they come fast and furious."

José lowers his gaze to the river. It's flat and calm. A garbage scowl moves against the current, toward Staten Island.

"You live around here?" the old man asks.

"Just a few blocks away. You?"

"Jersey City. Born here. Worked here. Retired here. And will be buried here."

José finishes his coke.

"I've been here a year."

"Like it?"

"It's nice."

"Oh yeah." The old man breathes. "Real nice. You can have it over there." He points to Manhattan. "It's way too busy for my taste. Shame what happened. I was sitting right here, on this very bench. Saw the whole thing."

José winces. Remembers where he was that day, when he learned his girlfriend was trapped inside.

"You wouldn't guess what I saw last night," he says, changing the subject. "I was riding my bike by the river and saw a whale. It jumped right out of the water. I'm not kidding."

"Was it big?"

"Huge. Brown as your shoes."

"I'll be damned. I know they're big fish in there. I saw a fin once, you know, a shark fin, come right up out of the water and cruise for a good ten minutes. It was right around when that shark movie came out."

"*Jaws*."

"Right, *Jaws*. That's when I saw my fin. No one believed me. They all say I had '*Jaws* fever.' Never saw it again."

"Probably retired to Florida," José jokes. He stands and stretches. "Nice talking to you. Hope you see that fin again."

"Maybe I'll see your whale. They're big fish out there. No one thinks so, but I do. There's sharks and whales and who knows what else in that river. You just got to look."

José is at the kitchen table when Reggie walks in.

"How was class?"

Reggie gets a Reese's from the freezer and sits down in a chair next to José.

"Terrible. A girl asked me why there are no more silversmiths like *Johnny Tremain*. Said it sounded like a cool job."

"What did you tell her?"

"I said the mechanisms of technology have made utilitarian artisans obsolete."

"How did that go over?"

"Mostly glazed looks. But then Timmy Higgins, the same kid who told me Britney Spears stole his copy of *Johnny Tremain*, said that his grandfather was a typesetter. And that he lost his job when computers came along. Then we talked about other jobs that have been lost over the years. Someone said her mom got replaced at Wal-Mart because they have a machine that checks people out."

"Sounds like a good discussion."

"It wasn't that bad."

"No one volunteered any insights into Johnny Tremain's sexuality?"

"No, but I was thinking about something. You know, at the end of the book, Tremain's hand finally opens up."

"I think I remember."

"It's only scar tissue keeping his fingers together. A doctor cuts them apart, and then Johnny can use his hand. Of course, he can't be a smith again. But he can shoot a gun for the Revolution. Even then they were setting the tone for mechanization. Johnny can't make a bowl, but he can pull a rifle trigger. And look at us now. We're a people of guns and weapons, not pots and pans."

"You're not bad a guy, Reggie. But you need a hobby."

José stands and heads out of the kitchen.

"Where are you going?"

"To take a ride."

"Say 'hi' from me to your whale."

He ignores Reggie's taunt.

José peddles fast. It's dark. The storm is coming. Racing up the Jersey coast. Sucking salt into its eye. It's all clouds. Black and heavy. Moving. The wind comes first. Smacks José in the face. Wobbles his bike. He hits the park and then onto the concrete path. The tick, tick, tick, tick of his tires drowned out by the whistling gusts. Sparks of lightning scar the sky. Too far away to hear thunder. But it's there. He whips the bike forward, side-to-side, like a slalom skier. The river is kicking up. A thousand white caps. Like miniature shark fins.

José stares into the water. Bringing it into focus. The whale is there. Amidst the white caps. He knows it. Can feel it. He bikes harder. Into the teeth of the wind. Bits of rain, just drops, sporadic, land on his forearms, run down his cheeks. They pick up, it starts coming down in sheets. Pelting. Cooling. Soaking. Clinging his clothes to his body. Like a tattoo. But still, he looks in the water. Riding. Looking for the flat swath. The still water. The whale.

A thunder cap echoes. Its partner, lightning, brightens the dark. The rain blinds him. He rips off his helmet and hurls it behind him. Gulps air. Grips his hands tight on the bike. Fuses them to the metal. Silver handles. No longer hands. Just bike and body and metal and skin and rain and clothes and air and sea and wind and rain.

A loud clap deafens him. It's like being next to an amp at a heavy metal concert. He eases up on his pedaling. Coasts. Rises up. Stretches. The muscles in the back, clenched tight in the cold rain, release. He's numb with the pleasure. And then, to his right, movement, a blinding flash of lightning that lifts him from the bike. He's airborne, defying gravity, and then slowly, as if descending a spiral staircase rung by rung, he lands in the river, spraying salt and water before finally coming eye to eye with his whale.

Acknowledgements

I BELIEVE in the wisdom that when it comes to life, the journey is everything, the end nothing. So it is with a collection of stories. The glory is in the process, the writing, where the concept and characters are culled from—that part of the brain where creativity mixes with memory, where doubt meets decision, and sadness intersects with joy.

But most importantly, the journey is filled with good and generous souls—friends and family, fellow writers, editors and publishers, those who provide a shoulder to lean on, who help to hone the work, who give unconditional support every step of the way. That's what really matters. The people by your side.

And so it is with *Automatically Hip*. There are many to thank, but I'll start with Vine Leaves Press: Jessica Bell, Amie McCracken, Peter Snell, and the rest of the team for championing my writing and giving it an opportunity to meet a wider audience. And appreciation to Kara Post-Kennedy, my editor at *The Good Men Project*, and to similar literary warriors at *Empty Sink Publishing*, *Smokelong Quartely*, *Haunted Waters Press*, *Work Literary Magazine*, and *Cigale*, magazines and journals which first published stories in this collection. Gratitude also to Jack Gwaltney, who partnered with me to create several stories which originally appeared in the Word Count Podcast.

Last, and always, love to my wife, Grace, who is strong and smart and everything to me.

Vine Leaves Press

Enjoyed this book?
Go to *vineleavespress.com* to find more.

CPSIA information can be obtained
at www.ICGtesting.com
Printed in the USA
LVHW091818230822
726678LV00005B/535

9 781925 965940